Copyright © 2011 by Raitetsu Media LLC and Ray Productions

All rights reserved. No part of this book may be reproduced, transmitted, or stored in an information retrieval system in any form or by any means, graphic, electronic, or mechanical, including photocopying, taping, and recording, without prior written permission from the publisher.

First U.S. edition 2011

Library of Congress Cataloging-in-Publication Data is available.
Library of Congress Catalog Card Number pending
ISBN 978-0-7636-5610-2

11 12 13 14 15 16 SCP 10 9 8 7 6 5 4 3 2 1
Printed in Humen, Dongguan, China

This book was typeset in CCLadronn Italic.

Candlewick Press
99 Dover Street
Somerville, Massachusetts 02144

visit us at www.candlewick.com

WWW.VERMONIA.COM

To the Pillar of Wind

Coming soon . . .

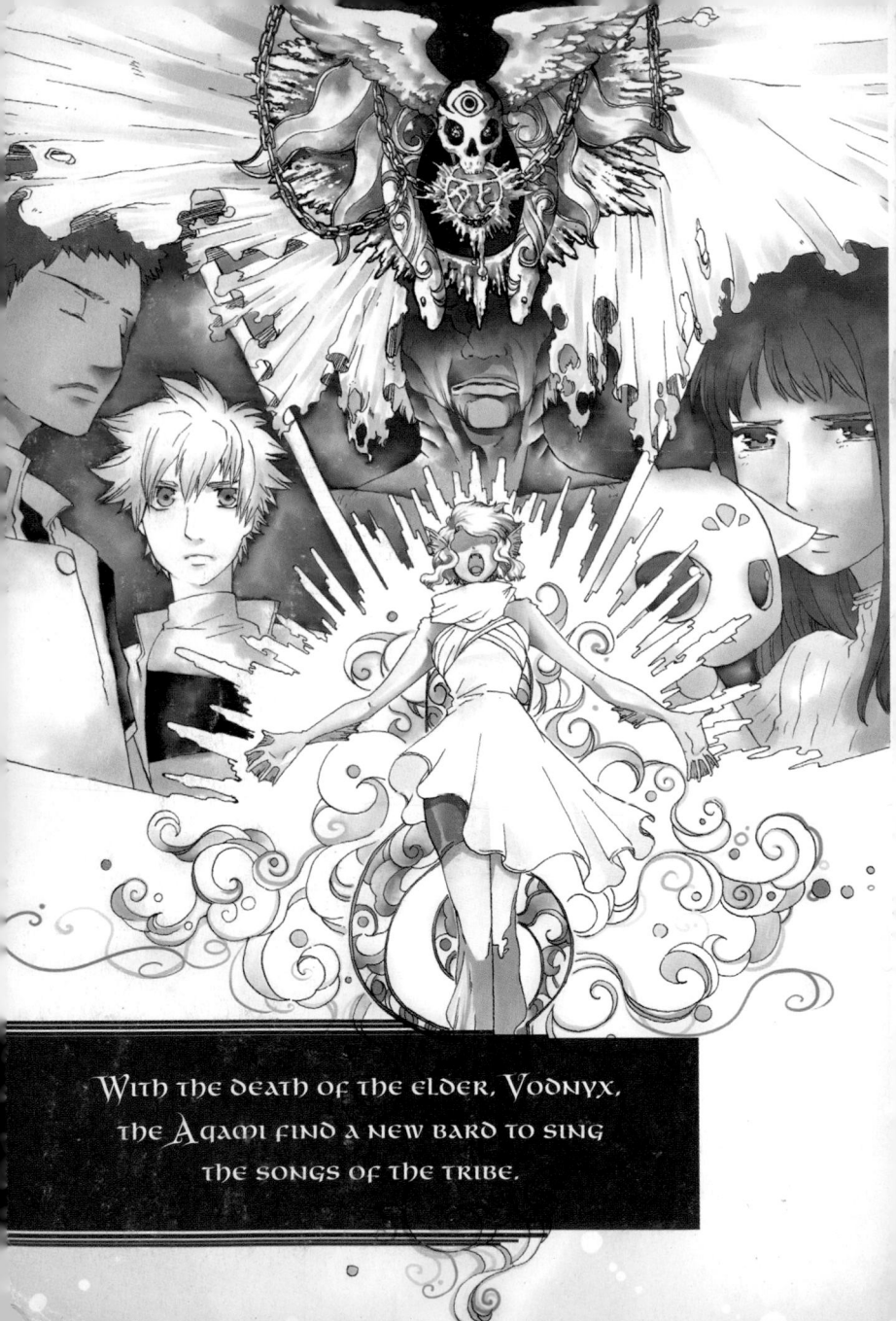

WITH THE DEATH OF THE ELDER, VODNYX,
THE AGAMI FIND A NEW BARD TO SING
THE SONGS OF THE TRIBE.

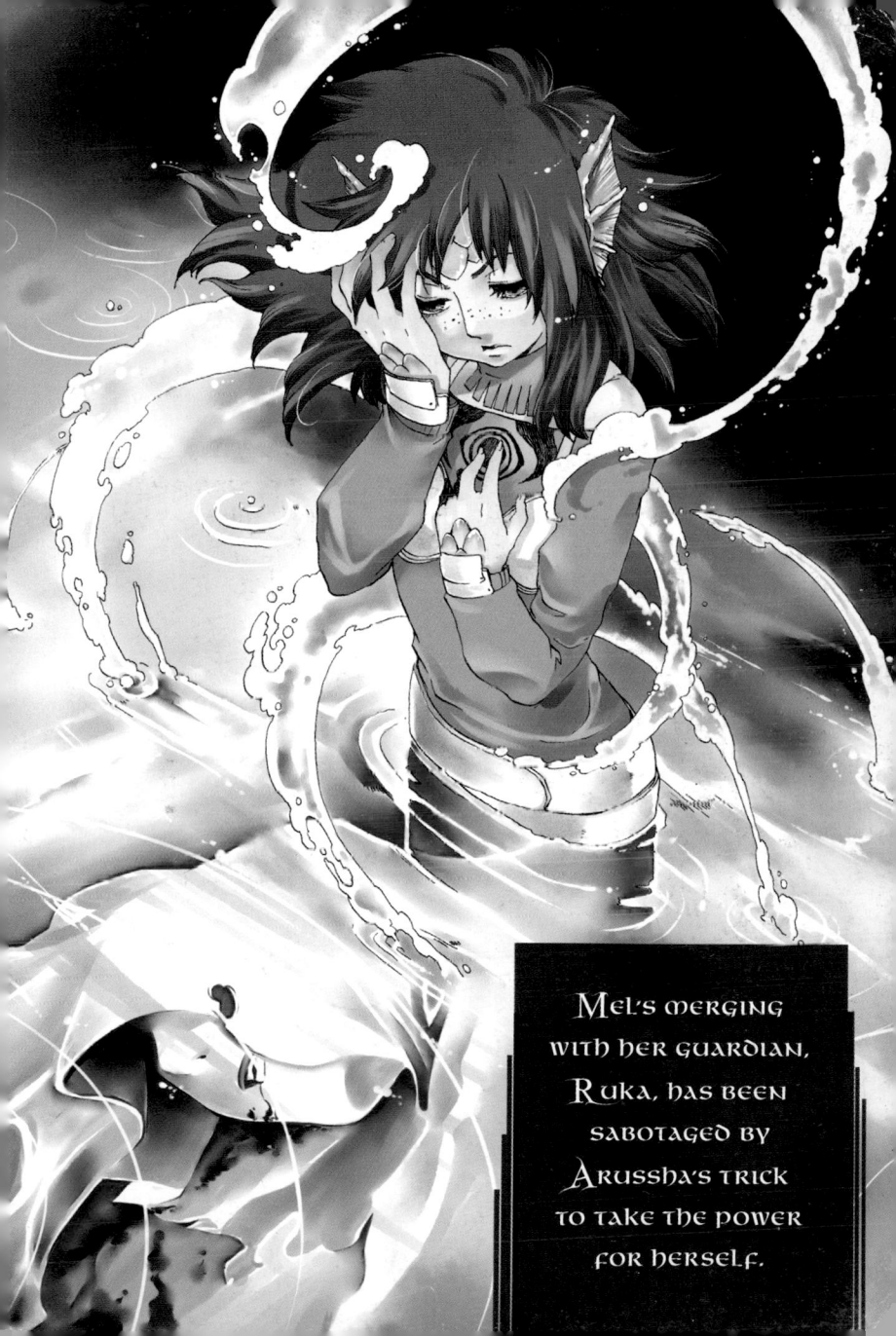

MEL'S MERGING WITH HER GUARDIAN, RUKA, HAS BEEN SABOTAGED BY ARUSSHA'S TRICK TO TAKE THE POWER FOR HERSELF.

RAINBOW, NAOMI, and KHANN are unable to save the PILLAR of FLAME from URO's soldiers, but MEL's sudden appearance raises doubts about her allegiance to the enemy.

JIM DOESN'T HESITATE TO RISK HIS OWN LIFE TO SAVE RAINBOW FROM DROWNING IN THE LAKE OF WISHES ON XANDAN ISLAND, HOME OF THE PILLAR OF THUNDER.

VERMONIA

THE WARRIORS' TRIAL

YOYO

CANDLEWICK PRESS

Jim
Bass Player
Blue Star Warrior

Rodvel
Uro's Loyal
Henchman

Arussha
Uro's Loyal
Dera

Mel
Lead Vocalist
Blue Star Warrior

Rainbow
Princess of the
Potonawi

**Captain
Acidulous**
Commander of
Uro's Forces

A civil war has destroyed the planet of Vermonia. The victorious army of General Uro has invaded the Turtle Realm to capture the Four Pillars and seize Queen Frasinella's sacred Bolirium. Only the Blue Star Warriors, Naomi, Jim, Doug, and Mel, four skateboarders from Union Middle School, stand in his way. Assisted by their animal guardians, Jim, Doug, and Naomi ally themselves with the peoples of the Turtle Realm to protect the Pillars, to defy Uro's dark Yami magic, and to release the imprisoned Mel.

In volume 4, Naomi and the Potonawi have failed to save the Pillar of Fire in the Chuwa Desert. Jim, Doug, and the squelp Satorin have rushed to the floating island of Xandan in an attempt to protect the Pillar of Thunder.

There, inside the island's core, Jim and Doug encounter trials that will push their warrior spirits to the limit.

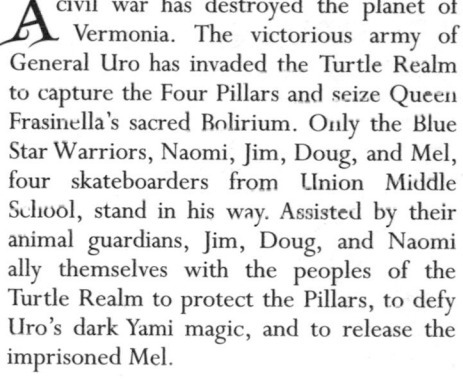

**General
Uro**
Master of Dark
Yami Magic

Satorin
Magical Squelp

Doug
Drummer
Blue Star Warrior

Frasinella
Queen of Vermonia

Fly
Potonawi Warrior

Naomi
Lead Guitarist
Blue Star Warrior

For more information go to vermonia.com

DOUG'S STRUGGLING.

JIM, HOLD ME.

BUT I JUST NEED A LITTLE MORE TIME.

I CAN'T BREATHE.

THAT'S IT.

HERE IT
COMES.

THERE'S NO WAY WHATEVER **THAT** WAS COULD HAVE SURVIVED.

DOUG!

OH, NO!

I FORGOT ABOUT ZANNI.

SHE WAS STILL DOWN THERE!

YOU'RE A REAL PAIN.

HUFF

THAT WAS A CLOSE CALL.

WHEEZE

DO YOU THINK I'M SUPERMAN?

SORRY, BUT THERE'S SOME WEIRD STUFF GOING ON.

I HOPE ZANNI GOT OUT IN TIME.

WELL, WE'RE GOING TO NEED WHATEVER YOU HAVE.

DOUG, DO YOU HAVE ANY OF RAITETSU'S POWERS LEFT?

NOT MUCH.

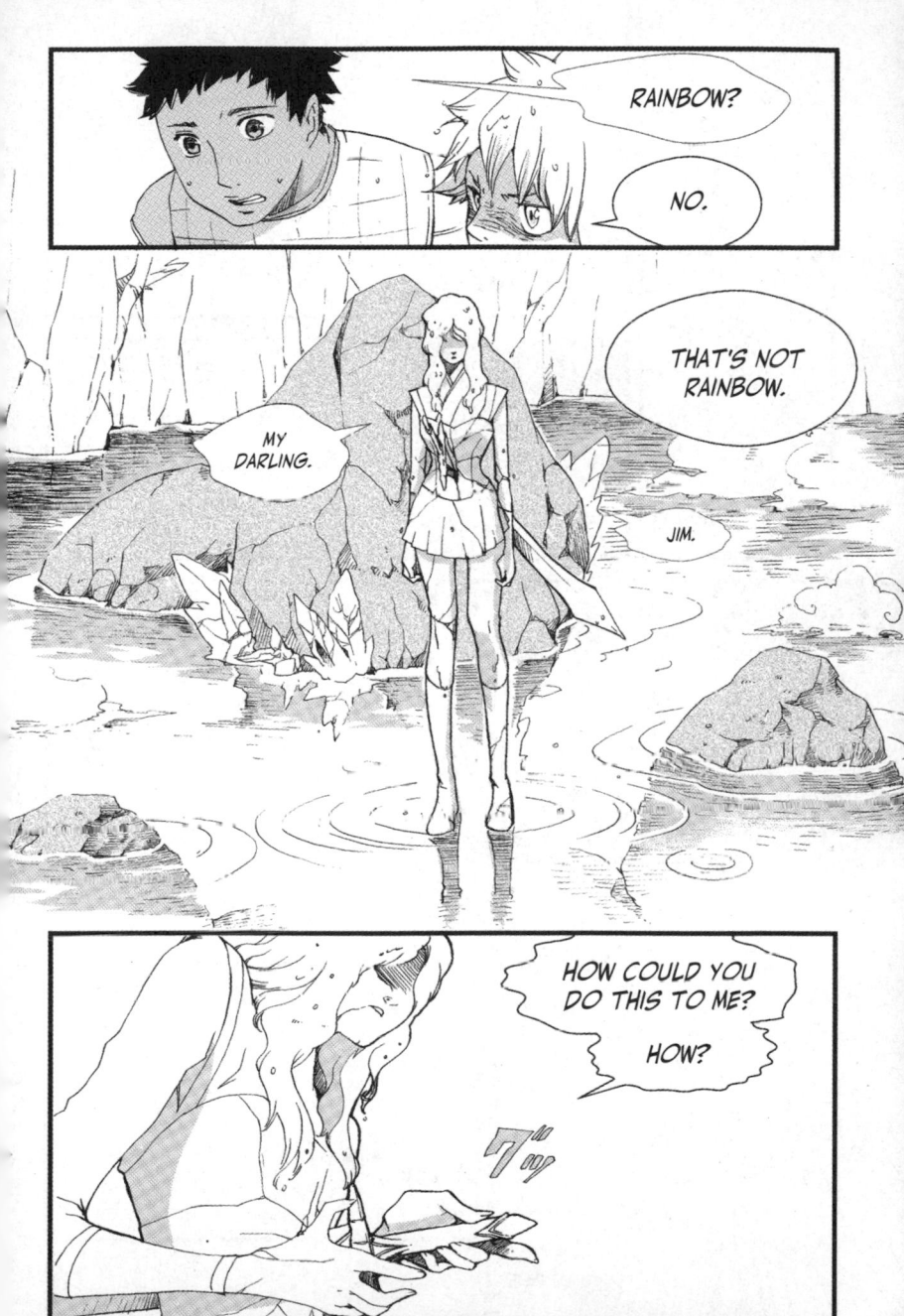

YOU'RE A FAKE.

RAINBOW WOULD NEVER HAVE ASKED ME TO DIE.

SO COME ON! SHOW ME WHO YOU REALLY ARE!

YOU REALLY WANT TO SEE? OK...

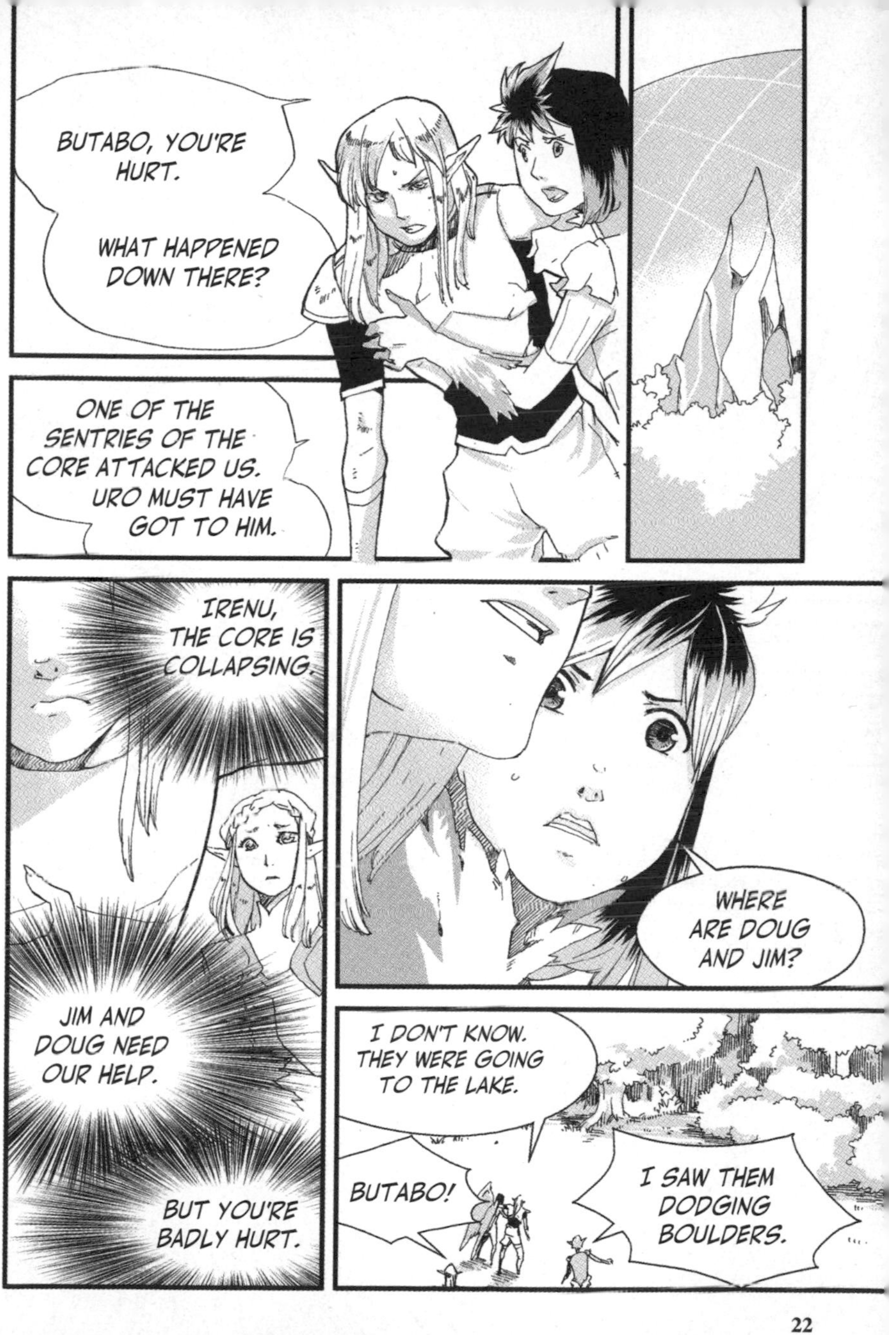

BUTABO, YOU'RE HURT.

WHAT HAPPENED DOWN THERE?

ONE OF THE SENTRIES OF THE CORE ATTACKED US. URO MUST HAVE GOT TO HIM.

IRENU, THE CORE IS COLLAPSING.

WHERE ARE DOUG AND JIM?

JIM AND DOUG NEED OUR HELP.

BUT YOU'RE BADLY HURT.

I DON'T KNOW. THEY WERE GOING TO THE LAKE.

BUTABO!

I SAW THEM DODGING BOULDERS.

WHAT'S GOING ON?

WHERE ARE MY POWERS?

HUH?

YOU MUST HAVE USED THEM UP FIGHTING IN THE DESERT!

INTRUDERS!

WE'LL FIGHT WITH YOU, NAOMI.

THANK YOU, MIRANDA...

KHANN...

THE AQAMI TOO!

OUR ONLY CHANCE IS TO OUTWIT THIS CREATURE.

JIM, ARE YOU OK?

NO, NOT REALLY.

JIM!!

AND SHE JUST KEEPS AT IT. LOOK!

EVERYTHING'S OK. DON'T WORRY.

I'M HERE TO HELP.

WHERE ARE THE OTHERS?

WHAT HAPPENED IN THE DESERT?

THIS DOESN'T FEEL RIGHT, DOUG.

.....

I KNOW.

COME ON, DOUG. TOGETHER.

ドッ

オ オ

WHAT ARE YOU GUYS DOING?

HEY!!?

?!?

STOP FIGHTING US. YOU'VE GOT TO UNDERSTAND–

WE'RE NOT HERE TO STEAL ANYTHING.

WE'RE NOT YOUR ENEMY.

OUR WISHES ARE THE SAME AS YOURS.

.....

BUT SHE SEEMS TO BE LISTENING...

JIM, STAND BACK.

WE WANT TO PROTECT THE ISLAND AS MUCH AS YOU DO...

SOMETHING'S NOT RIGHT...

YOU'RE RUTHLESS.

I ONLY WANTED TO HOLD YOU.

YEEEE!!

!!?

RAITETSU'S POWERS DEFEND ME.

IT'S NOT CLEAR TO ME. SOME POWER HOLDS US BACK, BUT I FEEL THAT MAYBE WE'RE GETTING CLOSER TO THE CORE...

I SENSE SOME OTHER FORCE IS AT WORK HERE, BESIDES THE ILLUSIONS.

WHAT DO YOU MEAN?

THAT'S GOOD NEWS IF IT'S TRUE!

YES! OK, THEN...

LET'S FOCUS ALL OUR THOUGHTS ON THE CORE. WE MUST MAKE OUR INTENTIONS KNOWN.

KEEP THINKING ABOUT THE CORE!

SO, GET READY!

PUSH THROUGH.

JIM?

I CAN FEEL SOMETHING TOO.

SO?

SECURE THE CORE.

WE'LL WAIT TO ATTACK THE CREATURE FROM HERE.

IT'S CHASING FLY INTO THE WOODS.

PERFECT.

NAOMI, REST. REGAIN YOUR STRENGTH.

BUT I WISH THERE WAS SOMETHING I COULD DO.

FLY WILL NEED MY HELP.

NAOMI...

IF THIS CREATURE'S MADE FROM MUD, THEN FIRE MIGHT TAKE IT DOWN.

...I THINK I HAVE A PLAN TO TRAP THE MONSTER.

HOW?

WE'LL TRY TO CREATE A HOOP OF FIRE TO TRAP HIM.

BURN THE WOODS?

MIKO AND I WILL MAKE IT FOLLOW US.

ONCE WE HAVE IT IN THE WOODS, KYUBI WILL USE HIS FIRE.

THE MONSTER WON'T BE ABLE TO ESCAPE.

OK.
NOW!

WHAT ARE YOU DOING TO MY TREES?

TAKE A GUESS.

KYUBI KNOWS WHAT TO DO.

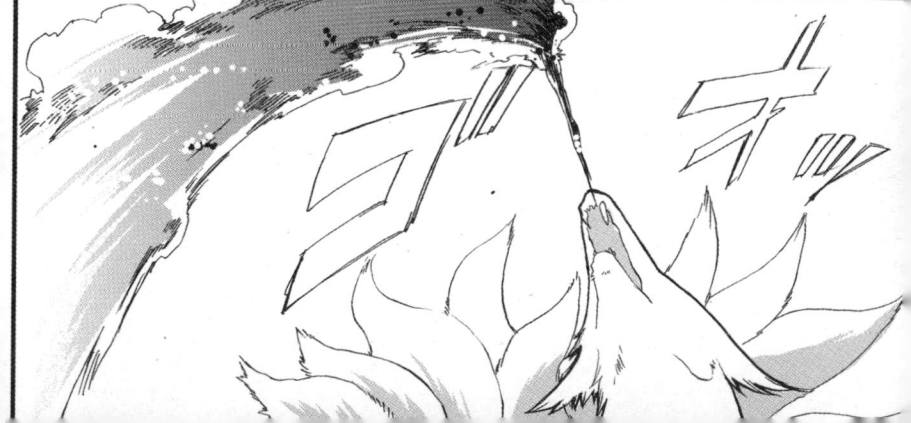

IT DOESN'T EVEN FEEL THE WHIP.

I HAVE TO FIND A WAY TO KEEP IT HERE.

.....

.....

WHERE DID IT GO?

RUNNING AWAY, STUPID?

ブオォォォ

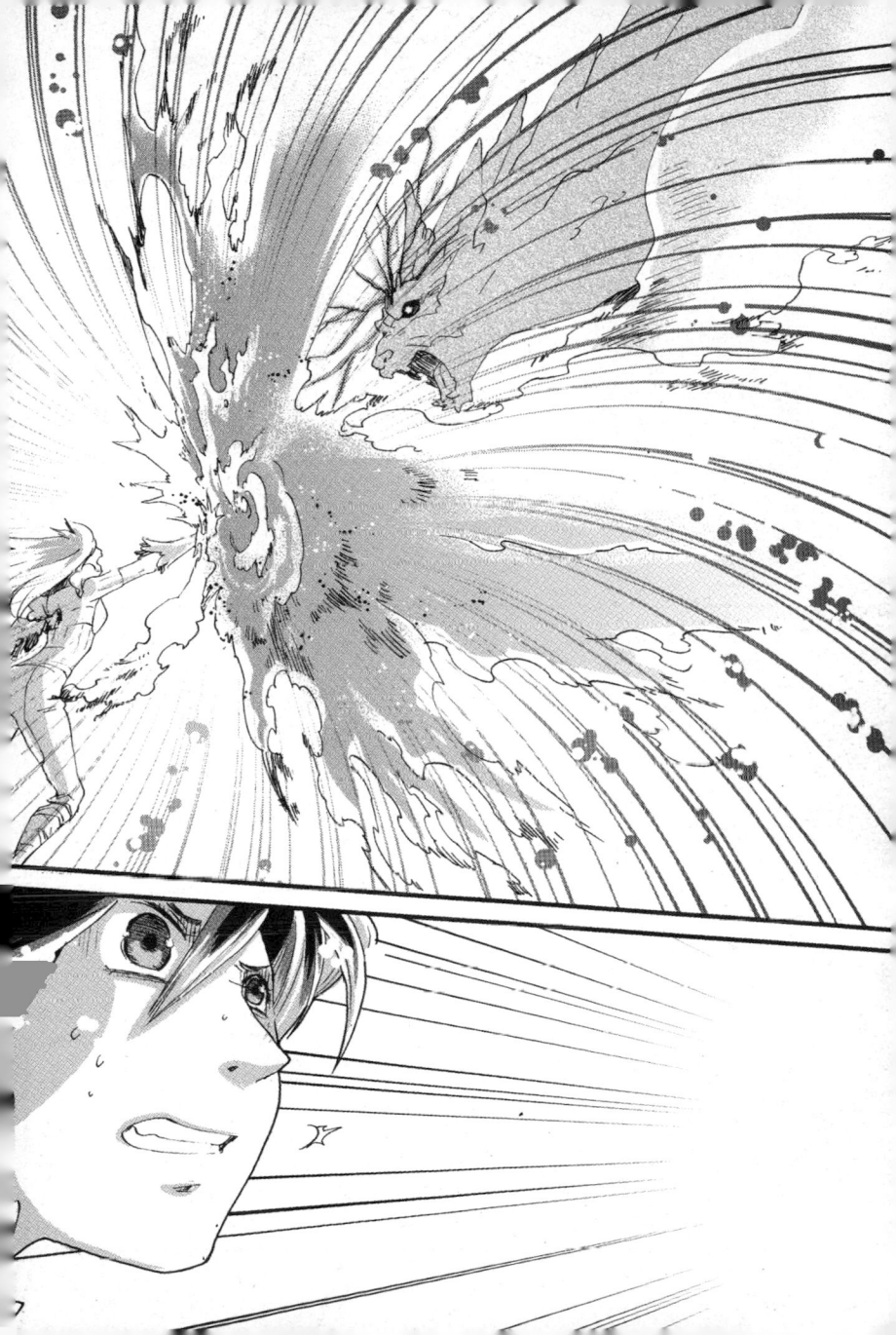

IT'S TOO STRONG FOR ME.

IT'S MOVING TOWARD IRENU.

I HAVE TO STOP IT.

URO NO LONGER CONTROLS ME.

AT LAST.

ブブッ

MAYBE I CAN STILL SAVE SOME PART OF MY ISLAND.

WHO AMONG YOU IS TRYING TO PASS THROUGH THE LAKE OF WISHES?

OUR FRIENDS DOUG AND JIM.

!!

I MUST STOP THEIR WISHES FROM APPEARING SO THEY CAN SECURE A CRYSTAL OF THE CORE. SOME OF THIS PILLAR MUST SURVIVE.

WAIT!

SATORIN...

JIM, WE HAVE TO GET OUT OF HERE.

BUT...!!

AND THEN LOOK FOR SATORIN TOGETHER.

WE GOT WHAT WE CAME FOR. NOW WE HAVE TO FIND THE OTHERS.

!!?

DOUG, I DON'T THINK I CAN GO ANY FARTHER.

WE'RE ALMOST AT THE TOP NOW.

DON'T LET GO.

OK. HANG ON.

ME TOO.

THAT WAS CLOSE.

PHEW!

!

NO KIDDING. I JUST HOPE THIS PIECE OF ROCK IS WORTH ALL THE EFFORT.

I'M EXHAUSTED.

LET'S HOPE WE DON'T HAVE TO FIGHT FOR A WHILE.

WHATEVER IT IS, IT'S COMING TOWARD US. RUN!

WHAT'S THAT?!

BUGS!

LEAVE THEM TO ME.

NOW WHAT?

JIM, RUN FOR IT!

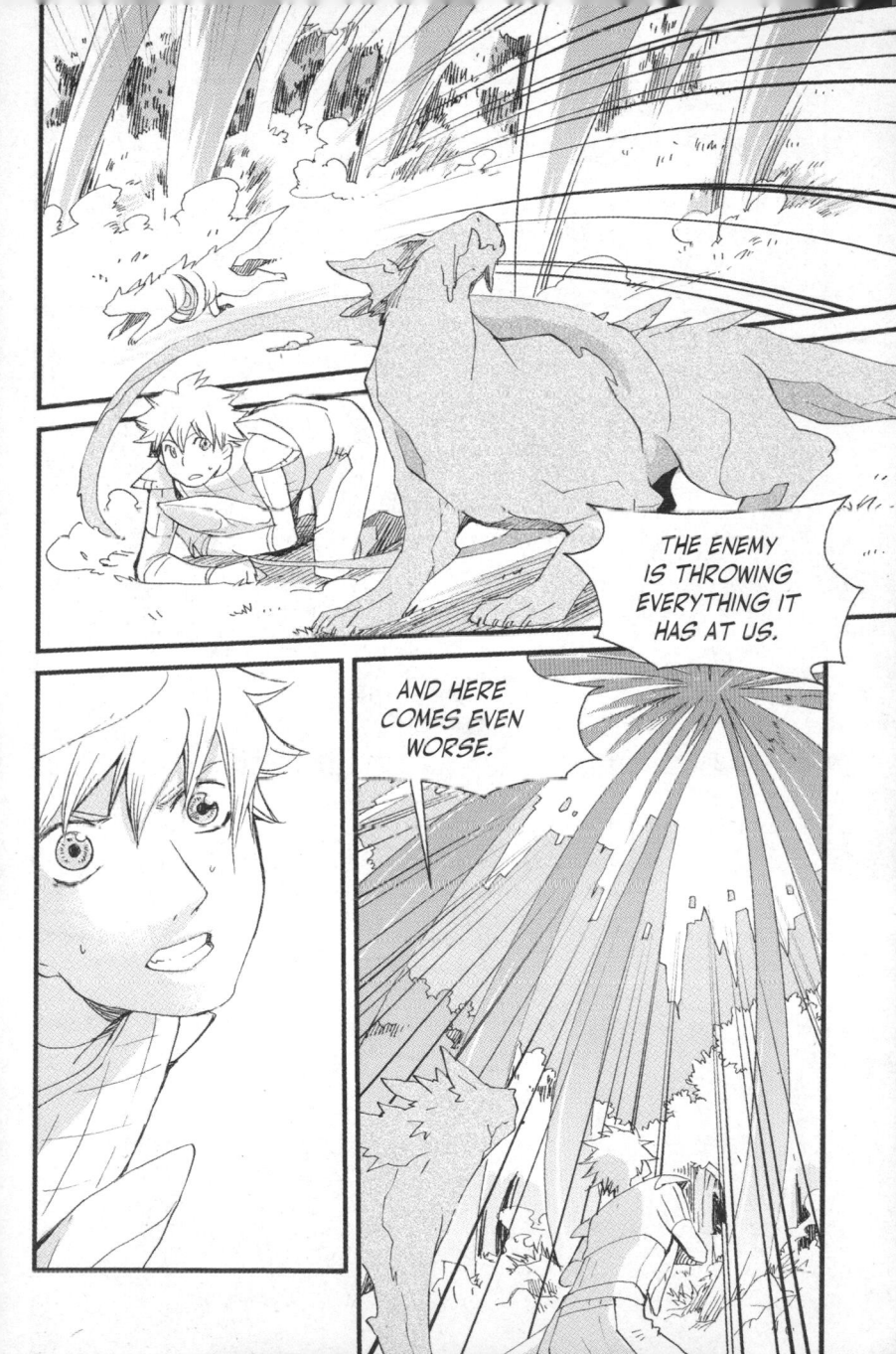

THE ENEMY IS THROWING EVERYTHING IT HAS AT US.

AND HERE COMES EVEN WORSE.

86

THIS LAST DEFENSE WON'T HOLD. YOU DON'T HAVE ANY CHOICE.

RAINBOW. IRENU.

GET OFF THE ISLAND. TAKE THE CRYSTAL WITH YOU.

THE SENTRY'S RIGHT, JIM.

NOW THAT THE SHIELD HAS BEEN BROKEN, WE'RE NOT SAFE.

ALL THAT MATTERS IS HOLDING ON TO THE CRYSTAL.

FLY AND BUTABO HAVE MADE A PORTAL OFF THE ISLAND.

DEMONS EVERYWHERE!

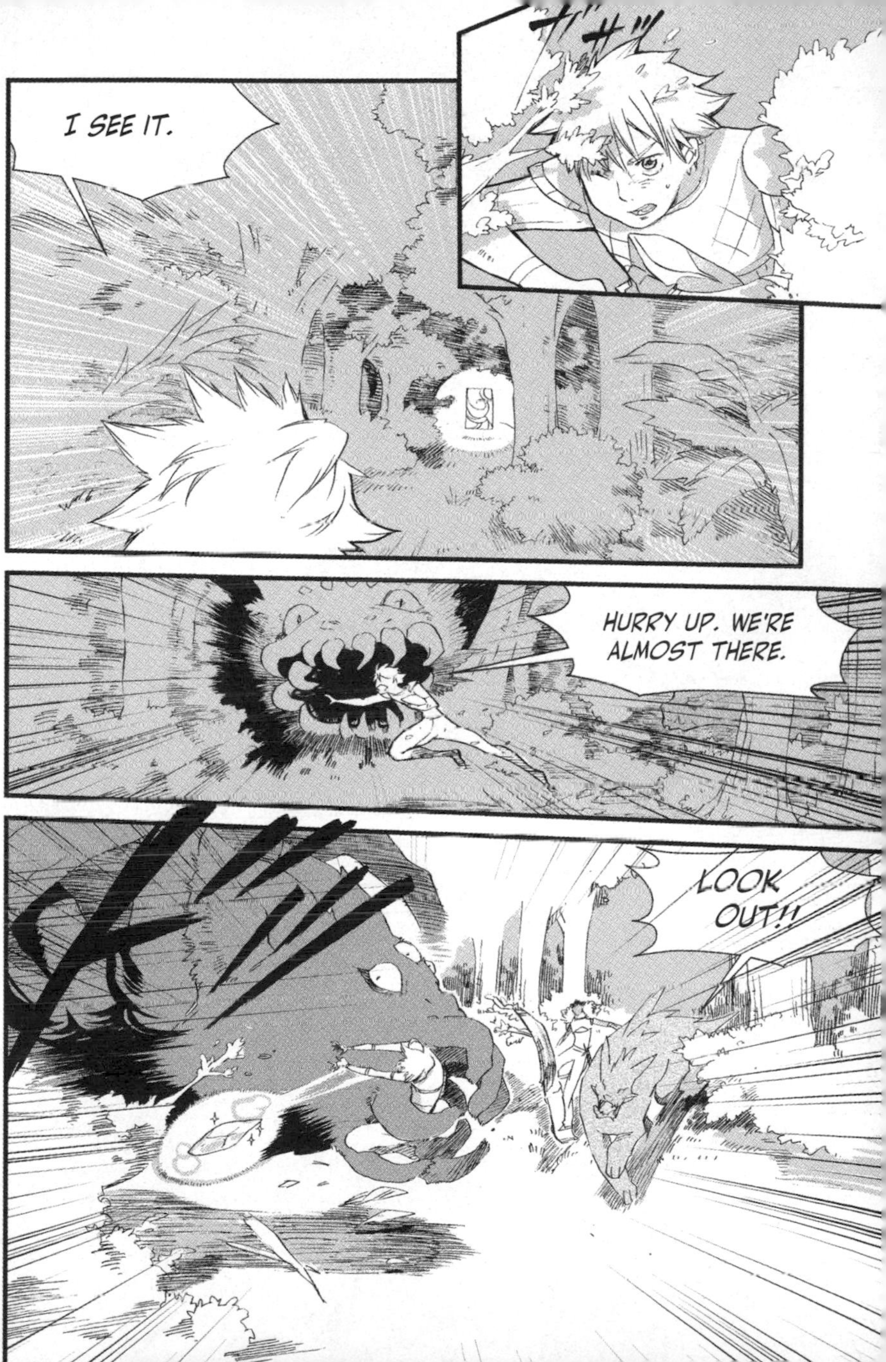

I SEE IT.

HURRY UP. WE'RE ALMOST THERE.

LOOK OUT!!

NAOMI, ARE YOU OK?

USE YOUR REMAINING POWER.

GET OFF THE ISLAND.

WHERE'S HE GOING?

FOR NOW.

THE GUARDIANS ARE GETTING BETTER AT MAKING THESE KIDS MORE POWERFUL.

SOON YOU WILL HAVE NO CHOICE.

YOU ARE NOT READY TO HEAR MY WORDS.

WE'VE LANDED?

THE VLESTE?

??

WELCOME ABOARD.
AM I HAPPY TO SEE
YOU GUYS!

NAOMI...?

.....

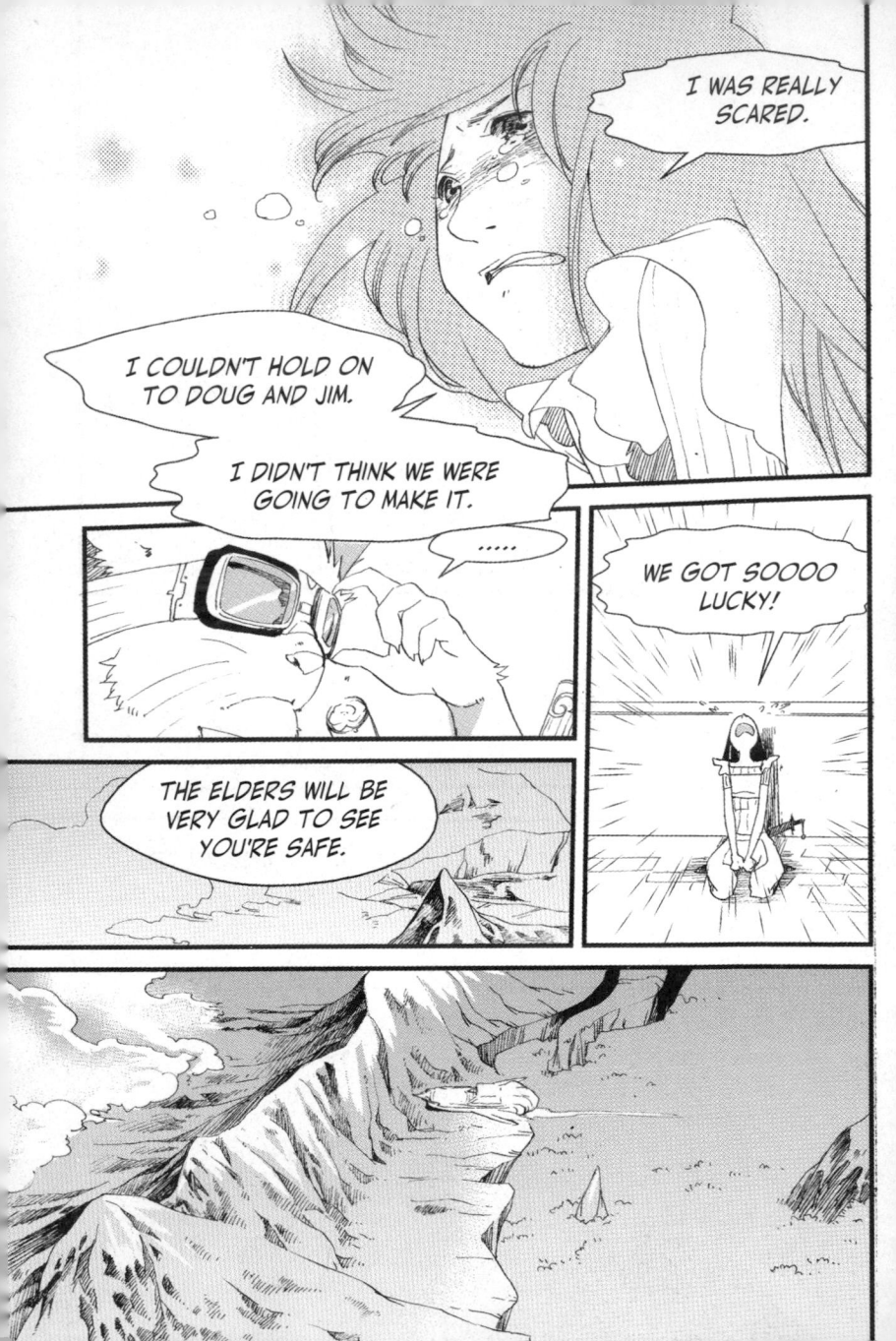

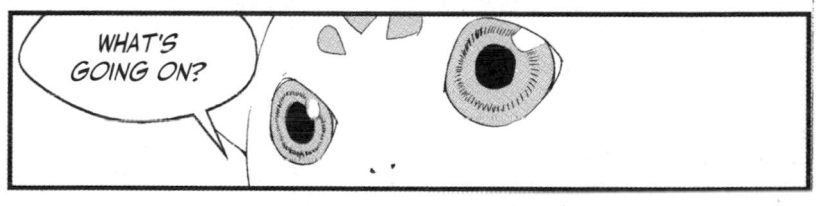

WHAT'S GOING ON?

WHERE AM I?

FOLLOW ME, AND WE CAN PICK IT.

I KNOW OF A SPECIAL FLOWER. WHEN YOU EAT IT, YOU CANNOT BE DECEIVED.

WAIT!

JUST LOOK AT ME!

I'M SATORAN!

I'M FROM YOUR SAME TRIBE.

HOW DO I KNOW THAT I CAN TRUST YOU?

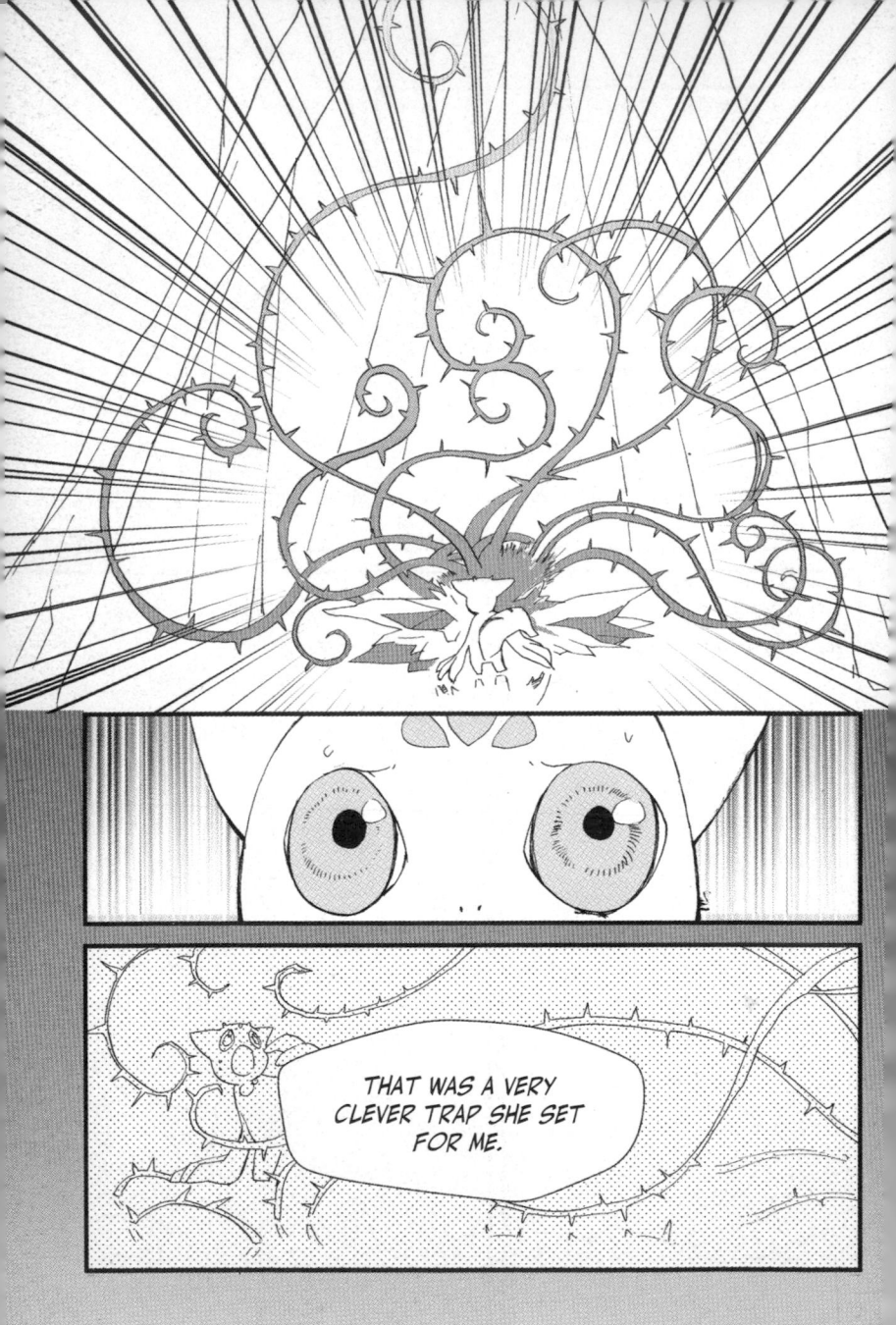

THAT WAS A VERY CLEVER TRAP SHE SET FOR ME.

HA, HA, HA, HA, HA.

SATORIN, YOU'RE SO GULLIBLE..

!!?

STOP THAT, SATORAN!

YOUR TRICKS AREN'T FUNNY.

WHO ASKED YOU?

!

...SQUELP.

NOW, AS FOR YOU...

.....

I DON'T KNOW WHY WE WASTE SPACE IN OUR PRISON.

WHAT A NUISANCE!

HOW COULD A PUNY THING LIKE YOU BE IMPORTANT?

I'M NOT IMPORTANT.
PLEASE LET ME GO.

MAYBE I WILL.

BUT FIRST I WANT SOME ANSWERS.

WHERE DID YOU COME FROM?

WHO SENT YOU TO BLUE STAR?

I DON'T KNOW.

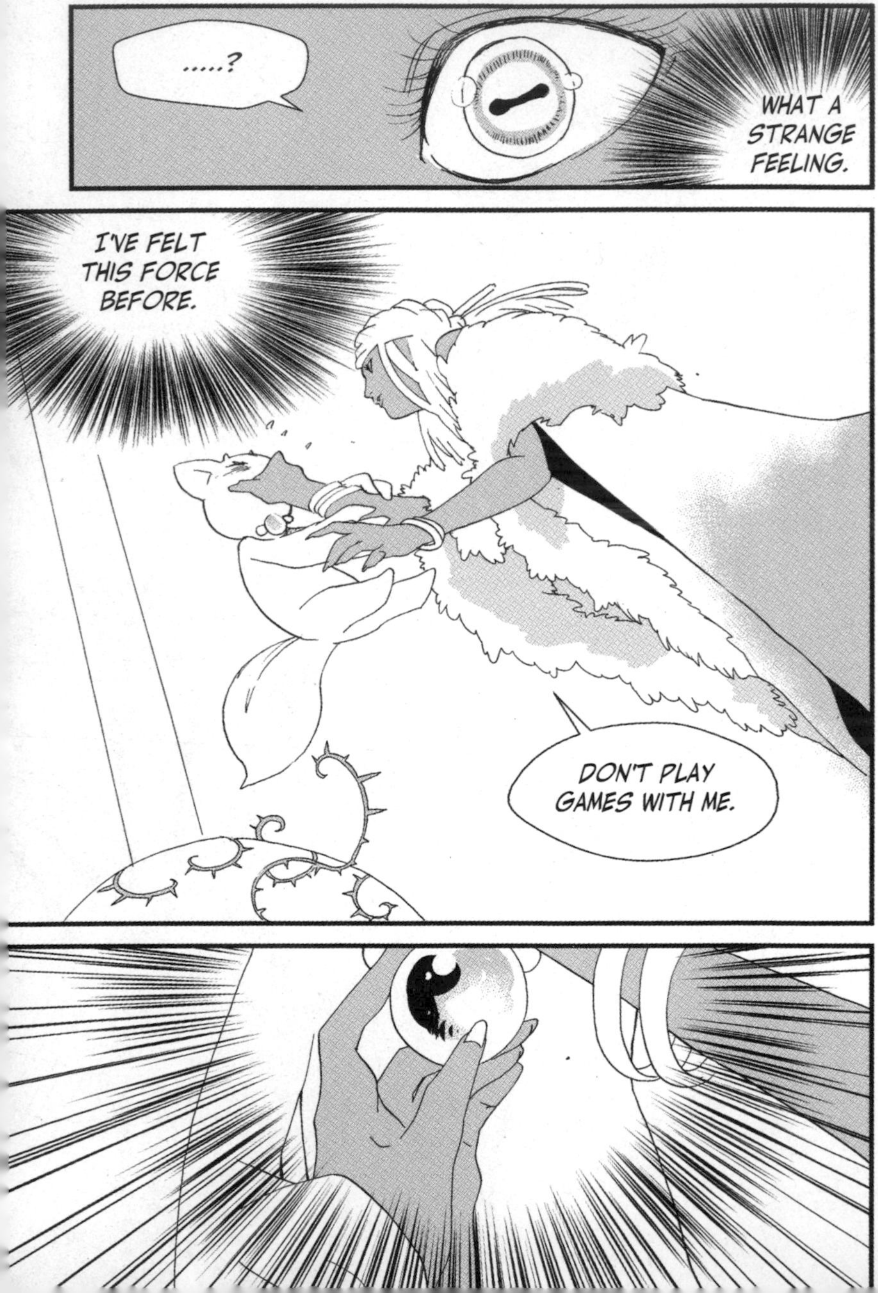

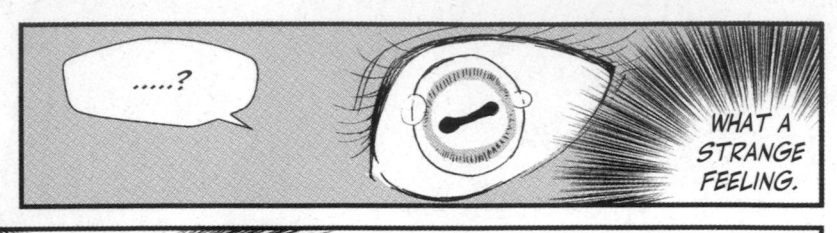

.....?

WHAT A STRANGE FEELING.

I'VE FELT THIS FORCE BEFORE.

DON'T PLAY GAMES WITH ME.

I DIDN'T TRY TO HURT HER.

HAAA.

WHAT AWAKENED RUKA?

I'M NOT SURE.

AS SOON AS I TOUCHED THAT CREATURE,

MORE OF RUKA'S SPIRIT OPENED INSIDE ME.

IT WAS LIKE AN EXPLOSION OF WATER FROM VERMONIA.

OVERWHELMING!

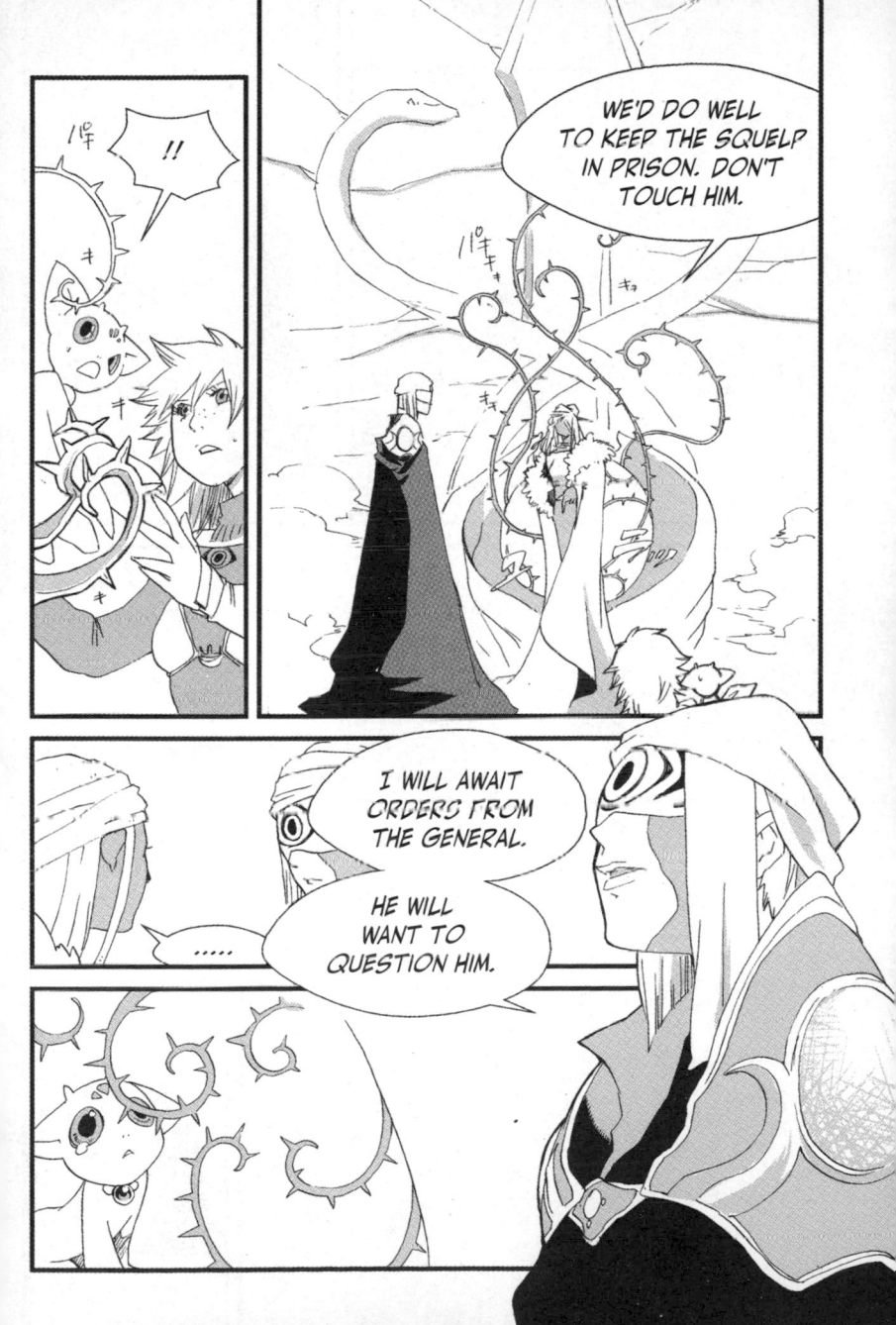

WHAT'S GOING TO HAPPEN WHEN WE'VE DESTROYED THE TURTLE REALM? WHERE DOES THE NEW ROAD GO?

YOU ONCE TOLD ME THAT I WAS CHOSEN TO BUILD A NEW ROAD TO A NEW WORLD.

.....

AND ONCE WE'RE THERE,

...YOU AND RUKA WILL BE FULLY MINE.

TO BLUE STAR, OF COURSE. TO THE PLACE WHERE YOU WERE BORN.

162

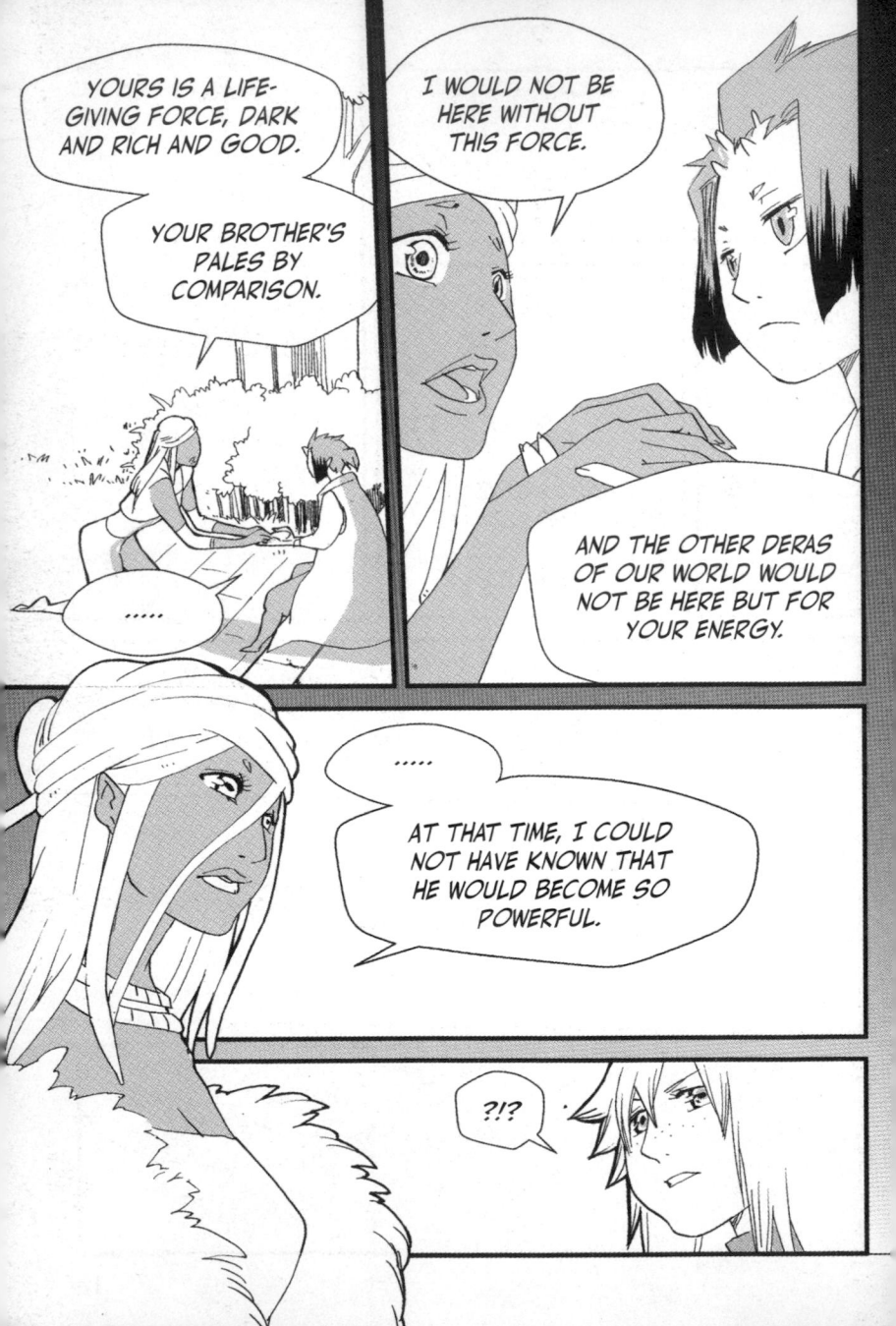

YOU WILL SOON.

I DON'T UNDERSTAND.

AND DON'T TRY TO ESCAPE. IT'S POINTLESS.

I NEED YOU TO GUARD THE SQUELP.

I HAVE TO GO.

I HAVE RUKA'S HEART SEALED INSIDE ME.

WHEREVER YOU GO,

I WOULD KNOW THROUGH RUKA.

GOOD-BYE, SWEET MELANIE.

NEVER FORGET THAT WE NOW SHARE A SPIRIT.

THEY'VE BEEN GUARDING YOU, TOO?

YOU'RE NAOMI'S FRIEND, AREN'T YOU?

.....

AND YOU CAN'T ESCAPE?

...I AM AFRAID

I AM BECOMING LIKE THEM.

IT'S IMPOSSIBLE.

WITH EACH DAY THEY CONTROL ME MORE AND MORE, AND NOW...

．．．．．

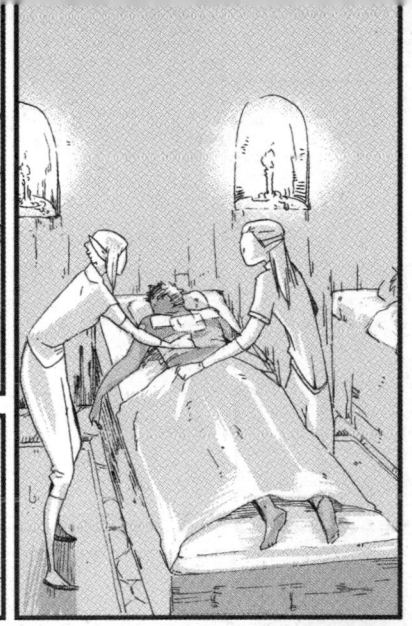

IS DOUG OK?

THANKS TO JIM'S POWERS, HIS WOUNDS ARE HEALING QUICKLY. HE NEEDS TO REST.

THAT'S GREAT.

NAOMI, YOU NEED REST, TOO.

YOU'RE RIGHT.

YOU HAD TO GO.

THE THREE OF US GOT BACK SAFELY.

AND DOUG AND JIM ARE GOING TO BE ALL RIGHT.

THERE WAS NO CHOICE. DON'T BLAME YOURSELF.

I'M FINE. I'LL HELP YOU.

THAT'S OK.

RAINBOW!

!

NAOMI, HOW DO YOU FEEL?

...THE WAY FLY'S BEEN LOOKING AFTER YOU.

I'LL LOOK AFTER JIM...

TAKE GOOD CARE OF HIM, RAINBOW.

I'M GOING TO GET SOME WATER.

ME TOO.

I'LL MAKE SURE HE'S SAFE.

HMM.

NOW ONLY DOUG NEEDS SOMEONE TO CARE FOR HIM.

?

ARE YOU SURE HE DIDN'T MAKE IT THROUGH THE PORTAL?

NAOMI, WHAT'S WRONG?

SATORIN!

!

LISTEN TO ME!

I'M SURE HE'S SAFE.

HOW WOULD YOU KNOW?

I JUST CAN'T BELIEVE HE'S NO LONGER WITH US.

SATORIN IS SAFE...

ZANNI?

SATORIN'S BEEN TAKEN PRISONER.

WHERE IS HE?

THEY'RE TAKING HIM TO URO.

IN THE ICE PALACE, BUT HE WON'T BE THERE FOR LONG. I OVERHEARD THEIR PLANS.

WHEN I KNOW MORE, I'LL RETURN.

WE HAVE TO SAVE HIM!

!

FLY!

WE CAN GET HIM BEFORE ANYONE NOTICES.

EXACTLY. IT'S SAFER THAT WAY.

YOU HAVE TO HELP ME RESCUE SATORIN.

JUST THE TWO OF US?

HE WAS... BUT NOT ANYMORE.

THAT'S STRANGE.

DON'T WORRY. HE'S PROBABLY JUST SLEEPWALKING.

I WONDER WHERE HE COULD HAVE GONE.

RAINBOW?

WHAT'S THE MATTER?

UGHH.